For William, Henry, Kim, and JoJo, with love

www.hmhco.com

The text of this book is set in Bembo Semibold.
The illustrations are mixed media.
Library of Congress Cataloging-in-Publication Data is on file.
ISBN 978-0-544-64811-1

Manufactured in China
SCP 10 9 8 7 6 5 4 3 2 1
4500602483

You have been my friend.
That in itself is a tremendous thing.
E. B. White

Henry & Leo

Pamela Zagarenski

Houghton Mifflin Harcourt
Boston New York

Henry could never say exactly what it was that made Leo different. Perhaps it was his glass button eyes, which made him look as if he knew secret things. Or maybe it was his jointed and movable parts. I guess we can never really know what makes one particular toy more special than another. But from the moment Leo was given to Henry on his second birthday, the two were inseparable.

Charlotte

One Saturday afternoon, Papa said, "Let's go to the Nearby Woods for a walk."

"Hurray!" said Henry. "Leo loves the woods."

“How can Leo love anything?” said Henry’s sister. “Leo is a stuffed toy, and toys ***aren’t real.***”

Henry let his sister believe what she wanted, but in his heart he knew differently. And as they walked through The Nearby Woods, Henry could tell that Leo loved hearing the birds and finding the woodland animals as much as he did.

The family walked until only a hint of the evening sun peered through the trees.

"We'd better start back," said Mama.

Henry was tired, so Papa carried him.

When they reached home, Henry woke just as Papa turned out the light. Immediately, Henry realized something was wrong.

"Papa, where is Leo?" he asked.

Henry and his family searched high and low, inside and out, but Leo was nowhere to be found.

"We will look again first thing in the morning," Papa promised.

"But Leo will want to come home tonight," said Henry. "We must leave a light on for him.

"Leo will be scared," Henry told his mother.

"Henry, Leo is not real. He is real only in your imagination," said Mama. "Why don't we imagine Leo tucked into a safe place? In the morning, we will go back to the Nearby Woods and find him."

Henry knew that his family just didn't understand what it truly meant to be real. To Henry, Leo was as real as his mother, his father, and his sister. As real as a tree, a cloud, the sun, the moon, the stars, and the wind. As real as a flower, a bee, a bird, a fox, a pebble, a brook, an ocean, or a whale. Leo was his best friend. Like a brother. They loved each other. They took care of each other. That's real.

LOVE

N
W
E
S

With the first hint of daylight, Papa, Mama, Henry, and his sister once again searched for Leo.

At first they saw nothing, but then . . .

"LEO!" Henry shouted.

"Thank goodness!" said Mama.

"But I looked in that very spot last night," said Henry's sister.

"That's strange," said Papa. "I'm positive I looked there too."

"You found home!" said Henry.
"I love you, Leo."

"I love you, too, Henry."